1. **This book may be kept three weeks. It is to be returned on / before the last date stamped below.**
2. **A fine of 20p will be charged for every week or part of week a book is overdue.**

For my father

Text copyright © 1997 Roy Apps
Illustrations copyright © 1997 Amy Burch

The right of Roy Apps to be identified as the author of this work
and the right of Amy Burch to be identified as the illustrator of
this work has been asserted to them in accordance with the
Copyright, Designs and Patents Act 1988.

This edition first published in Great Britain in 1997 by
Macdonald Young Books, an imprint of Wayland Publishers Ltd

Typeset in 15/22 Veljovic Book by Roger Kohn Designs
Printed and bound in Belgium by Proost N. V.

Macdonald Young Books
61 Western Road
Hove
East Sussex
BN3 1JD

British Library Cataloguing in Publications Data available

ISBN 0 7500 2155 1
ISBN 0 7500 2156 X (pb)

A CAMP TO HIDE
King Alfred

ROY APPS

ILLUSTRATED BY AMY BURCH

MACDONALD YOUNG BOOKS

1

A Secret Place

The crisp winter sunlight had given way to a chill evening mist, which hung like a thick curtain over the hidden waterways and islands of the Somerset levels.

One of these islands was tucked away behind tall reeds and rushes. It could only be reached by a small rowing boat. From under a tent of willow branches on this island a thin wisp of grey smoke curled upwards until it was lost in the mist.

Sitting by the fire was a boy called Wulfric. This was his secret place. No one else knew about it or how to get to it. It was where he carved wood into spears, lit fires and cooked fish he'd caught in the river. It was the only place where he could get away from his younger sister Eadgifu.

Wulfric gazed into his fire and like all twelve year old Saxon boys, dreamt of leading an army of local men to fight with King Alfred, just like his father had once done.

Then he dreamt about sailing his rowing boat on the sea – which he had never seen, but which he'd been told was a mass of water as far as the eye could see.

By the time Wulfric put out his fire and rowed back through the rushes towards home, it was dark.

"Wulfric! You were told to be back before sundown! You idle your life away in a dream, child!" scolded his father.

Wulfric sighed. When I'm leading an army for King Alfred, he thought, no one's going to call me child or tell me what to do anymore.

"We still have much to do to prepare for our Twelfth Night revels," said his father. "Now go and help your mother and Eadgifu with the bread."

Twelfth Night was Wulfric's favourite feast. A whole pig was spit-roasted and the winter's cold, long, dark nights were soon forgotten amid singing, laughter and wine.

He watched his father's servants chattering excitedly as they prepared for the great feast. Everyone agreed that this was going to be the best Twelfth Night ever. Times were good. King Alfred of Wessex had paid the Viking marauders gold to secure his people a lasting peace.

Nobody gave the Viking 'slaughter-wolves' a second thought.

2
Wynflaed's Dreadful Tale

Wulfric sneaked a mouthful of mead from his father's drinking horn and poked out his tongue at Eadgifu's disapproving look. He was enjoying himself.

Then came the knock at the door.

Not a gentle knock, but a furious,
frantic hammer with two fists, that made
the tapestries shake and the candles stutter.

Instinctively the men reached for their
weapons.

His sword at the ready, Wulfric's father
edged open the door.

In stumbled a wild-eyed youth; his cloak shredded, his hair matted with dark blood, white frost glistening on his eyebrows. He stood there blinking in the bright firelight.

"My name is Wynflaed. Which of you is Aelfwin, master of this Hall?"

Wulfric's father stepped up to the stranger. "I am Aelfwin, thane of King Alfred. Speak to us Wynflaed, without fear or favour."

Everyone stood round the mysterious stranger. The minstrels had stopped singing; food and flagons of wine lay untouched on the table. The only sounds were of the crackling fire and the dogs snoring under the benches.

Quietly; tremulously, as if he wished with all his heart that he did not have to say the things he was saying, Wynflaed began his dreadful tale...

"I have ridden from Chippenham."

"But that's four hours ride! No wonder he looks so cold!" murmured Wulfric's mother. "Eadgifu, girl, fetch him mead!"

Wynflaed drank the goblet of mead as if it were water. He wiped his lips. "Good people of Somerset, the time for making merry is past. Tonight the town of Chippenham has been laid to waste, our homes razed by fire, our kinsfolk killed."

Wynflaed paused, tears of anger swelling in his eyes. "The Viking slaughter-wolves have attacked again...!"

A dreadful, disbelieving hush filled the hall. Did the gold Alfred had paid the Vikings count for nothing?

Then Old Eadwig, Wulfric's uncle, voiced an even greater fear. "Chippenham is King Alfred's winter home. What has become of him?"

"Through God's mercy, he made good his escape," said Wynflaed.

There were muffled cries of "Amen", from around the hall.

"Aelfwin, I must talk with you alone," said Wynflaed, urgently.

Wulfric's father took Wynflaed out across the courtyard to a small bower.

In the hall, the guests gathered in grim-faced groups, musing on the dreadful news, unable to enjoy the revels anymore. Only his younger sister, Eadgifu, noticed Wulfric slip out.

"You dare say anything...!" threatened Wulfric.

"You'll be in trouble if father catches you," was his sister's sullen reply.

Wulfric stood at the entrance to the bower, listening to his father and Wynflaed.

"While Alfred lives," Wynflaed was saying, "there is hope for our kingdom. But the Vikings are already on his trail; he needs a hiding place. Somewhere so secret, that not even local people know of it, for not every wain is a loyal subject of the King."

Wulfric's father sighed. "It's difficult to think of anywhere..."

Without a moment's hesitation, Wulfric strode into the bower. "I know of such a place," he said.

3

A Camp To Hide King Alfred

Wulfric's father jumped up. "Wulfric! Out of here before I throw you out!"

"Let the boy speak," said Wynflaed.

Wulfric told his father and Wynflaed about his camp.

"Who else knows of this place?" asked Wynflaed.

"Only me. And you and my father now," said Wulfric.

"Then we have no time to lose," said Wynflaed. "Follow me."

In the stable, an old man in a ragged, hooded tunic was brushing down a couple of horses. He was stooped low, so that Wulfric could not see his face. He made Wulfric feel uneasy.

"Old Hereberht here rode with me," said Wynflaed. "Show him your place, boy and he will decide if it's fit enough to hide the King."

But Wulfric's father didn't like the look of the old man either. "Is he to be trusted?" he whispered.

"There's no wain in Wessex more loyal to our King," said Wynflaed.

And so, excited but fearful, Wulfric led the old man Hereberht out of the courtyard and across the fields to the marshes.

It was cold, dark and foggy. Once, old Hereberht lost his footing on the unfamiliar track and Wulfric grabbed his hand before he slipped into the water. He was surprised by how strong the old man seemed.

They sat in Wulfric's boat, old
Hereberht's weight making the tiny craft
sit dangerously low in the water. The old
man said nothing, but Wulfric could sense
him listening all the time, for the sound of
Viking voices across the marshes.

Wulfric paddled the boat skilfully through the thick rushes to his secret camp, wondering whether the Vikings had reached his home; wondering whether the old man would think his camp fit for the King.

"It is a most remarkable place," said old Hereberht when they finally reached Wulfric's camp.

"Will it suit the King?" asked Wulfric.

"Indeed it will," said old Hereberht. "Oh yes. This will suit King Alfred."

"Are you sure?" asked Wulfric, hardly daring to believe the old man's enthusiasm. "I mean, hadn't you best go back to wherever the King is hiding and ask him?"

"There is no need for that young Wulfric," said the old man. "I *am* King Alfred." And he pulled off a ragged mitten to reveal a silk glove. Then he eased off the silk glove to reveal a ring. Even in the uncertain flickering firelight, Wulfric could make out the words *Alfred Rex* – King Alfred.

Wulfric was at a loss as to what he should do or say. He stood up; then he knelt down. Then he stood up again. "Sire..." he mumbled.

"Enough of that, Wulfric," said the King. "Go back to your father Aelfwin's Hall and tell my trusty henchman, Wynflaed, that your secret place is indeed a camp to hide King Alfred."

4

The King Prepares

When Wulfric got home, the first chill light
of dawn had already broken through the
sky. Everything was quiet though, the
Vikings hadn't reached the marshes – yet.

"Wulfric, you are best placed to take
food and provisions to the King," said
Wynflaed, next day, "for a *boy* wandering
about the marshes won't arouse suspicion."

The Vikings came that morning. Not
an army, but half a dozen burly thugs on
horseback. They came across Wulfric on
the edge of the marsh, on his way to see
the King.

"Where y'going boy?"

Wulfric remembered Wynflaed's words, *'a boy won't arouse suspicion'*. He would be a boy all right.

"I'm going to my castle!"

The men guffawed. "Ooo... where's y'castle then, m'lord?" asked their leader, sarcastically.

"Over there," said Wulfric, pointing in the opposite direction to his secret camp. More guffawing.

"Leave him be," said another of the
Viking soldiers. "He's only a boy. What will
he know?" And off they rode, jeering.

It wasn't until they were fully out of
sight that Wulfric realised he was shaking
like a leaf.

Over the next few weeks, small groups of Vikings rode round the villages and Halls, looking for King Alfred. After a few weeks, they took their search elsewhere.

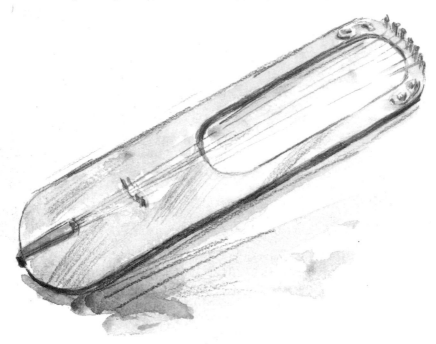

The rumours about the King's whereabouts were many. One of Wulfric's friends told him he knew for sure that the King was travelling the kingdom of Wessex, disguised as a minstrel.

Another had heard that he was most definitely staying with an old lady and had burnt her cakes. Wulfric said nothing; just nodded as if he believed every word.

Wulfric would visit the camp during the day. His rough willow tent was now covered with wattle and daub and lined with thick fur skins. A roaring fire burned constantly.

Wulfric was no longer shy in the King's presence, but chatted with him like he might to a kindly uncle.

"I enjoy your company, young Wulfric," said the King.

Once Wulfric had shown them the way, Aelfwin and one or two other thanes would visit the King at night. They were making plans, Wulfric knew. Plans to do battle with the Vikings when the King judged the time to be ripe.

Wulfric's home became increasingly busy. Neighbouring earls and thanes would come, and then go. Aelfwin would ride off for days at a time.

"What's he like, the King?" asked Eadgifu, wide-eyed.

"Honestly Ead! You're not meant to know about it!"

"I'm not stupid," retorted Eadgifu.

As the damp greyness of winter gave way to spring, Wulfric knew that the time for revenge was drawing near.

One day, he was about to make his regular journey to his secret camp, when a familiar figure rode in to the courtyard. It was Wynflaed. He dismounted and spoke to Aelfwin. Then he ran across to Wulfric.

"Wulfric! Tell the King that every earl and every thane in the kingdom of Wessex now have their militia ready."

The first flowers were beginning to bloom in the water meadows as Wulfric rowed the King back through the rushes towards home.

"Wulfric," said the King. "I want you to be part of my company when we march on the Vikings."

Wulfric felt as if this was the most exciting day in the whole of his life.

The feeling didn't last for long, though.

"Wulfric? Marching against the Vikings? But he's only a boy, sire!" Aelfwin protested to the King. "His mother will need him here."

"Wulfric is my subject, but he's your son, Aelfwin my thane. If you forbid that he comes with us, then so be it."

Wulfric sat at the edge of the courtyard, prodding the ground angrily with a stick, watching the men load horses and wagons for the long march against the Vikings.

He felt someone behind him. He looked up and saw Eadgifu. "Go, Wulfric. You have spent most of the winter with the King after all. I'll explain to mother. Go on, big brother!"

Wulfric slipped under the covers on the back of a large wagon. There was a sudden lurch and he caught a glimpse of his sister's wave as the wagon began to roll away.

5

Face To Face
With The Vikings

"Wulfric! You have disobeyed me!"

"I know father. But I have obeyed my King."

There was little that Aelfwin could say to that.

And so, in the seventh week after Easter, Wulfric rode with his King against the Viking army at Edington.

The fighting was fierce. As the day wore on, Wulfric's helmet weighed on his head and his sword grew heavy in his hand.

But in the end, the Vikings fled.

For two weeks Alfred's army lay siege to the Viking camp, then on the fourteenth day a solitary figure tramped wearily out of the Viking camp towards Alfred's tent.

It was Guthrum, the Viking King.

"Alfred, King of the people of Wessex, I come to you in all humility. We have no wood to burn, no food to eat. My people are cold, hungry and frightened. I come to make peace, on your terms."

The peace was made. Guthrum and his Vikings withdrew from Wessex.

Alfred's weary, but triumphant soldiers began to make their various ways home. It was the moment Wulfric was dreading.

"Are you ready to come back to Somerset?" Wulfric's father asked him, as they loaded their wagons. Then he paused. "Or are you ready to do fulltime service for your King?"

Wulfric was speechless.

"You're man enough to make the decision for yourself," said Aelfwin.

And so it was that Wulfric, found himself riding along with King Alfred, towards Wessex's southern coast.

"One of the plans I made while hiding in your camp, Wulfric, was to make sure that Wessex would never again be attacked by marauders from the sea. I am going to create an army of the sea. Soldiers in boats will guard our lengthy coast."

They rode on to the top of a hill.

"Have you ever seen the sea, Wulfric?"

Wulfric shook his head. Then he looked down. Beyond him, glistening in the afternoon sunlight as far as the eye could see were the white-topped waves of the English Channel.

"Are you still prepared to serve me, Wulfric?" asked King Alfred.

"Yes sire," said Wulfric, his voice full of excitement and pride. "I am happy to do whatever you wish."

"Then would you be prepared to sail a boat as one of my first sea soldiers, Wulfric?"

Wulfric thought of the days he had spent in his camp, dreaming of the sea. And he could think of no better thing; than to sail a ship for Alfred, his King.